Acknowledgment to Burkhard Sievers for his contribution
to the conceptualization of this book;
and Kane/Miller's thanks to Jeff Whisenant for his role in
making us aware of the book.

First American Edition 1999 by Kane/Miller Book Publishers
Brooklyn, New York & La Jolla, California

Originally published in Germany under the title *Ich Heibe José Und Bin
Ziemlich Okay! (My Name's José and I Think You'll Like Me!)*
by Peter Hammer Verlag GmbH, Wuppertal, Germany, 1996

Copyright © 1996 Peter Hammer Verlag GmbH
American text copyright © 1999 Kane/Miller Book Publishers

Library of Congress Cataloging-in-Publication Data

[Ich heibe José und bin ziemlich okay! English]
I'm José and I'm okay : three stories from Bolivia / ideas and illustrations by Yatiyawi
Studios ; story realization by Werner Holzwarth ; translated by Laura McKenna. —
1st American ed.
p. cm.
Summary: A scrappy eleven-year-old orphan works hard at his
uncle's tire repair shop and proves himself at work and in a bicycle race.
PZ7.H74365Jo   1999   99-17618

ISBN 0-916291-90-1
Printed and bound in Singapore by Tien Wah Press Pte. Ltd.
1 2 3 4 5 6 7 8 9 10

I'M JOSÉ AND I'M OKAY

(Three Stories From Bolivia)

Story Realization by Werner Holzwarth

Idea and Illustrations by Yatiyawi Studios

Translated by Laura McKenna

KM Kane/Miller Book Publishers

Brooklyn, New York & La Jolla, California

José the Prankster

José's favorite place was black, round, seven feet high and smelled like rubber. It was the big pile of tires in the corner of his Uncle Ramos' auto repair shop. That's where José worked, and that's where he was one morning not so long ago.

It was ten after ten in the morning and time for a break.

"The Bolivars are

"José, where are you hiding?" called his Uncle Juan Ramos. He always did that just when José would be daydreaming about the *Bolivars,* his favorite soccer team.

"Get down from there. Your break is over!" growled Juan Ramos.

Although José was barely eleven years old, he already understood a lot about working in a garage.

"Come on now! How about checking the pressure of that tire!"

"And bring me a number 14 wrench and a new exhaust for the Jeep," Uncle Ramos yelled. "Done, Boss."

"And check the tire pressure on the motorcycle!" "It's fine."

"Connect up the battery cable!"

"Already did it, sir."

"Well then, sweep up the garage. It has to look neat and tidy for the customers."

José's Uncle Ramos was tough, but also fair. And strong.
That came from doing hard work, which was why his
muscles were as large as a weight lifter's.

"I'll do it if you want, Boss!"

But today Juan Ramos had a problem.
"Darn! This screw is stuck! I can't get it off!"

"Can I give you a hand?" asked José.

"YOU? Help ME?? That's a laugh."

"I'm the boss! You got t

José knew exactly what to do to loosen a frozen screw.
He put one arm of a lug wrench over the screw and then
attached a thick pipe over another arm of the wrench.
Then he jumped onto the pipe with both feet. The screw came loose.

"That kid's something else!" thought Juan Ramos.

"I'm the best!" thought José.

Then — and who could say for what possible reason —
when his uncle walked by him, José stuck out his foot.

"He's the boss, so nothing'll happen to him" thought José.
But Uncle Juan went sailing right into a pile of tires.

"The next time you send me flying like that, I'm going to send you flying . . .
right out the door!" shouted his uncle. "What you just did was wrong!"

"Hey! Everybody makes

"He's right, though" thought José.
"I was wrong. But how I got that screw
off was absolutely right."

José the Winner

José had only been in the town of Sorata an hour when he found out from his aunt that there was going to be a big bicycle race. So now here he was in the shed looking for his uncle's old red bike.

"It doesn't have any brakes!" warned Aunt Esmeralda.

"What do I need

If you brake, you lose!"

"Besides, it's too big for you," continued Aunt Esmeralda.
"When you sit on the seat, your feet hardly reach the pedals!"

"Then I'll just put blocks of wood on them," said José with a laugh.
"And how are you even going to get onto it?" asked his aunt.
"All I need is a big rock," he replied.

"I can't wait for the race to start!"

Over twenty riders were lined up at the starting line. Most were much bigger than José.

And almost all of them made fun of him. "Hey, Shorty!" they yelled.
"This isn't a race for shrimps. Why don't you go back home to your mama?"

José didn't show them how mad he was, but he was glad when the race got started.

To José, the houses just seemed to fly by.

José rode very well. With only a few miles to go to the finish, only one rider remained ahead of him.

José was gaining on the leader. But just as José was about to overtake him, he kicked at José's bike!

"If he'd gotten me, I'd be in a ditc

José swerved away just in time. So, instead of kicking the bike, the lead rider kicked the air. He lost his balance and fell off his own bike.

right now!"

With just a hundred feet to go, José's legs were pumping like pistons. All the hard work he'd done at the garage was paying off.

"I don't believe it!

I really DID it!"

José threw his hands up over his head. Then he shrieked, remembering that he had no brakes!

Seconds later, José jumped off and let the bike keep going. He landed with a thud.

"No big deal.

I finished first!"

"Well kid, you taught us a lesson!"
said the guy who finished second.

"I don't know why we ever called you 'Shorty,'
because you're a giant!" said the third place
finisher, and he laughed.

"Aunt Esmeralda will never

believe th

"You didn't do so bad yourself!" answered José.
He couldn't wait to see the look on his aunt's face.

José the Avenger

It was a day when there was more work to do in the garage than usual. But the only one who seemed to be doing any work was José.

"They're in there having a party while I'm out here workin

Is tha

While loosening the lug nuts on a truck, he could hear his uncle, the boss, along with a couple of his old friends, playing music in the office and laughing. And as José struggled with the tire, the sweat pouring off him, he heard them start singing.

"José, get some beer. We're dying of thirst!" shouted his uncle.

José took the empty bottles and ran down to the
corner store for the second time that day.

He came back, gave his uncle the beer and
went back to work. He took care of some new
customers and changed a few more flat tires,
all the while doing the work of three
people. And they were in there drinking for ten!

"No, this is NOT right!"

"José! More beer! We need a lot more beer!"
That was the last straw.

"Get if yourself, you gorillas! I have too much to do!" José shouted.

He got a slap for saying that, and it hurt. And he still had to get
the beer. In fact, he went many more times that day.

"This is anything bu

kay!"

Finally it was the end of the day.
José was still miserable.
He sat in his favorite place,
the pile of old tires, and cried.

"They have me do all the work! They think they can do this to me just because I don't have a mother or father to stand up for me!" said José to himself. Slowly his pain and sorrow turned to anger and then rage.

"They're gonna pay for this! I'm gonna get revenge!" José promised himself. "I'm gonna lock them up and let them suffocate from the smell of their own beer breath!"

"I hope they choke to death!"

José jumped down from the tire pile,
closed the door of the office,
put two big locks on it and skipped away,
whistling to himself.

"Very slow

v, please!"

He felt more convinced of the correctness of his actions than ever.
"I hope they die a slow death from their own stink!" José murmured.

But gradually his anger subsided.
And the more calm he became, the more scared he felt.

"What if they really do suffocate?"
José asked himself. "They're so
drunk now, they won't realize they're
running out of air! They'll die and
not know what hit them!"

"They might be dead

Slowly and silently, José sneaked back into the shop.
His hands trembling, he removed the locks, and, using
all his strength, managed to push open the door to the
office. Out came a stench worse than a hundred pounds
of smelly cheese. And there was a noise that sounded like
three buzz saws going at once. But José was happy.
He'd never smelled a sweeter smell nor heard a lovelier sound.

"Snoring can be the most beautiful sound in the world!"